D0586755

60000338889

ORCHARD BOOKS
338 Euston Road, London NW1 3BH
Orchard Books Australia
Level 17/207 Kent Street, Sydney, NSW 2000
A Paperback Original

First published in 2015 by Orchard Books

© 2015 Rainbow Magic Limited.
© 2015 HIT Entertainment Limited.

HiT entertainment

Rainbow Magic is a trademark of Rainbow Magic Limited.
Reg. U.S. Pat. & Tm. Off. And other countries.

Illustrations © Orchard Books 2015

A CIP catalogue record for this book is available
from the British Library.

ISBN 978 1 40833 647 2
1 3 5 7 9 10 8 6 4 2

Printed in Great Britain

MIX
Paper from
responsible sources
FSC
www.fsc.org
FSC® C104740

The paper and board used in this paperback are natural recyclable
products made from wood grown in sustainable forests. The
manufacturing processes conform to the environmental regulations
of the country of origin.

Orchard Books is a division of Hachette Children's Books,
an Hachette UK company

www.hachette.co.uk

Heidi
the Vet
Fairy

by Daisy Meadows

ORCHARD

www.rainbowmagic.co.uk

The Fairyland Palace

Heidi's Vet Surgery

Heidi's Vet Surgery
All Animals Welcome

Weatherbury Vet Surgery

Kirsty's Hou

Wetherbury Village

Jack Frost's
Ice Castle

Jack Frost's
Folly Vet Surgery

Wetherbury Vet Surgery

The High St.

Jack Frost's Spell

The fairies like to fuss and fret
That one must train to be a vet.
Exams are hard and tests are tough.
I want to skip the boring stuff.

But Heidi's things give instant skill
To treat all creatures who feel ill.
I stole each one and that is how
The Frosty Vet can see you now!

The Pink Stethoscope

Contents

Surgery Assistants

Rachel Walker opened her eyes and saw the early-morning sun making shadow patterns on the ceiling. For a moment she couldn't think why she felt so excited. Then she remembered. Today, she and her best friend Kirsty Tate were going to work in a vet's surgery. She sat up and looked across the room. Kirsty was still fast asleep in her bed.

"Wake up, Kirsty!" said Rachel,
swinging her legs out of bed. "I can't wait
to see all the animals!"

Kirsty sat up and rubbed her eyes. Then
she gave a huge smile.

"I was dreaming that we were vets," she
said. "Today is going to be so much fun!"

Rachel was staying with Kirsty for half term, but they hadn't expected her visit to be quite so exciting. On the first day of the holiday, Kirsty's next-door neighbour Lisa had popped round to ask them an important favour.

Lisa was a vet, and she had just opened her own surgery in the village. She had arranged for some local journalists to come for an open day, so they could write reviews in their papers. She was hoping that they would say good things in their reports so that people would bring their animals to her.

Lisa had asked Rachel and Kirsty if they would help her out on the open day. They were going to take care of the journalists as they looked around the surgery. The girls would be making cups of tea and coffee, serving sandwiches and other refreshments, and keeping the waiting rooms nice and tidy.

"It was kind of Lisa to have uniforms made in our size," said Rachel as she pulled on the blue tunic with its white logo. "We're really going to look like part of the team."

"I think that being a vet must be one of the best jobs in the world," said Kirsty. "I'd love to spend every day helping poorly animals get well again."

"I hope that the journalists say nice things about Lisa's surgery," said Rachel. "It's very useful to have a good vet nearby."

She stroked Kirsty's pet cat, Pearl, who gave a loud purr.

"Pearl agrees!" said Kirsty with a laugh.

"I hope that we get to spend some time with the animals too," said Rachel. "I wonder what different sorts of pets we'll meet."

"A kangaroo would be fun!" said Kirsty.

"Or a dolphin," said Rachel, with a secret smile at her best friend.

Kirsty smiled back.
She guessed that
Rachel was
remembering
the wonderful
adventure they
had shared with
Ally the Dolphin
Fairy and her dolphin
friend Echo. Ever since they had first
met on Rainspell Island, they had made
many fairy friends and had lots of happy
adventures together.

After breakfast, the girls pulled on
their shoes and hurried next door. Lisa
answered their knock.

"Good morning, girls!" she said in a
cheerful voice. "Are you looking forward
to today?"

"Very much!" said Rachel with a big smile. "What sort of things will you be showing the journalists?"

"They'll start by observing some of my examinations," said Heidi. "Then I'll give them a tour of the building, ending with a visit to the recovery room."

It was a short walk from Kirsty's road
to the surgery. Lisa opened up and pulled
on her white vet coat. Then she picked up
a small box and took the girls out to the
front of the surgery.

"This box is full of balloons," she said.

"I'd like you to blow them up and tie them to the railings. I want everyone to know that this is a special day!"

Balloon Surprise

Rachel and Kirsty each took a balloon.

"Thank you, girls," said Lisa. "When the journalists arrive, please show them into the smallest waiting room and let me know they're here."

She went inside and the girls began their task. Soon there were lots of colourful balloons bobbing from the railings.

"Those look very jolly!" said a voice.

The girls looked up and saw a small group of men and women walking towards the surgery. The man in front had a camera around his neck, and he used it to take a picture of the girls and the bright balloons.

"They must be the journalists," Kirsty whispered.

Rachel gave them a big smile.

"Welcome to Wetherbury Vet Surgery," she said. "Please follow me – I'll take you to the waiting room."

Rachel led the group of journalists into the surgery while Kirsty stayed outside. She noticed that two of the journalists at the back were very short compared to the others. They were wearing baseball caps and holding a camera and a press pass up to their faces, so she couldn't see what they looked like.

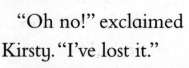

Kirsty was tying a knot
in the last balloon when
Rachel came back
out of the surgery. At
that moment, the wind
caught the balloon and
carried it high up into
the air.

"Oh no!" exclaimed
Kirsty. "I've lost it."

"I don't think so," said Rachel,
looking up and shading her eyes. "Look –
it's floating down towards you again."

"But that's impossible," said Kirsty. "I
hadn't finished tying the knot – how can
it still be full of air?"

The girls watched in amazement as the
blue balloon sank lower.

"There's something dangling down

24

from it," said Rachel. "You must have tied the string on already, Kirsty."

"I really didn't," said Kirsty, squinting as the sun shone in her eyes. "Rachel, that's not a piece of string hanging from the balloon. It's a fairy!"

Rachel glanced around, but it was still early and there was no one else around. The fairy landed on the railings and waved her wand, scattering sparkling fairy dust through the air. A piece of string coiled around the neck of the balloon and then tied itself to the railings.

The fairy smiled at the girls. She was wearing a blue coat a bit like Lisa's and she had a super-blonde pixie haircut which gleamed in the sunshine.

"Hello, Rachel and Kirsty," she said. "I'm Heidi the Vet Fairy."

"It's lovely to meet you, Heidi," said Kirsty. "Welcome to Wetherbury!"

"Thank you," said Heidi. "This is my first-ever visit to the human world. I'm glad I found you so quickly."

"Have you come to look at Lisa's new surgery?" Rachel asked.

Heidi shook her head.

"I know all about it, of course," she said. "My job is to watch over all human vets and to take care of animals in Fairyland."

"Goodness, you must be very busy!" said Kirsty.

"Yes," said Heidi. "My surgery is always bustling with patients – until this morning."

"What happened this morning?" asked Rachel.

"When I arrived at my surgery, there wasn't a single animal in the waiting room," said Heidi with a worried frown. "That has never happened before. There's always at least one, and usually more. I went to check on my magical objects, and they had been stolen!"

The girls gasped.

"I keep them in a display cabinet in the surgery," Heidi went on. "Someone had smashed the glass and taken everything.  Who could have done such a terrible thing?"

Rachel and Kirsty exchanged a knowing glance.

"This sounds just like one of Jack Frost's mean tricks," said Kirsty.

"But why would he want my magical objects?" asked Heidi. "And what has he done with my patients?"

Pet Problems

"I don't think Jack Frost needs an excuse for causing trouble," sighed Rachel. "He just does it because he enjoys it."

"The Magical Animal Fairies thought that you might be able to help me," Heidi went on. "I must find my magical objects soon, or things will start to go wrong for vets in the human world."

31

"We've promised to help our friend Lisa today," said Kirsty. "But we will do everything we can to help you, too."

"Thank you," said Heidi. "Oh, I think Lisa's first patients are arriving. I'd better hide!"

She slipped inside Rachel's tunic pocket as a slim man strode towards the surgery with a brown-and-black dog.

"Good morning!" he said to the girls. "My name is Mr Gilmore. My dog Maddie hasn't been eating her food, and she is very quiet. I'd like the vet to take a look at her, please."

"Of course," said Rachel. "Follow us and we'll take you straight through."

The girls led Maddie and Mr Gilmore into the patients' waiting room. Then Kirsty went to knock on the door of Lisa's examination room.

"Your first patient has arrived," she said.

"Please bring them in, and fetch the journalists too," said Lisa, smoothing down her white coat.

Rachel led Maddie and Mr Gilmore into the examination room, while Kirsty went to get the journalists. Soon they were all standing around Maddie, who was sitting on a table in the middle of the room.

"Hello, Maddie," said Lisa in a friendly voice. "Are you feeling a bit poorly? Let's see if we can find out what's wrong."

She ruffled the dog's silky ears, and Maddie looked pleased.

"She knows you're trying to help her," said Mr Gilmore with a smile.

Murmuring comforting words to her patient, Lisa started her examination by checking inside Maddie's ears. Everyone waited to hear what she would say.

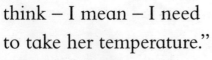

"Lisa looks a
bit nervous all
of a sudden,"
Kirsty
whispered to
Rachel.

"Er… um…"
Lisa muttered. "I
think – I mean – I need
to take her temperature."

She took out her thermometer and
dropped it.

"Butterfingers!" called out one of the
journalists with a giggle.

Lisa picked up the thermometer and
took Maddie's temperature. She looked
inside her ears again.

"You've already looked there," called
another journalist in a mocking voice.

"Oh," said Lisa, blushing. "Yes, sorry. I must be more nervous than I thought."

Kirsty looked around and saw that the journalists who had spoken were the short ones she had noticed earlier. They were holding their hands up to their faces and laughing at Lisa.

"Her nose is very runny," said the first journalist. "Perhaps it's a virus."

"Yes, in her stomach, I'd say," agreed the second journalist.

"Um, yes, possibly… I just need to double-check something," Lisa stammered.

"Those two journalists are making Lisa nervous," Heidi whispered to Rachel. "You have to get them out of here, or Maddie might not be diagnosed correctly."

"Would you all like some tea and biscuits?" Rachel asked the journalists at once.

The journalists all agreed eagerly and Lisa gave the girls a grateful glance.

"Follow us back to the waiting room," said Kirsty.

They had avoided trouble for now, but why was Lisa finding it so difficult to diagnose Maddie? It wasn't a very good start to the open-day visit!

Tea and Disguises!

The girls hurried into the small staff kitchen. Rachel started to make tea, while Kirsty opened some packets of biscuits and arranged them on plates.

"Is it safe to come out?" Heidi whispered.

"Yes, no one will disturb us in here," said Kirsty.

The little fairy
fluttered out of
Rachel's tunic
pocket and
perched on
the rim of a
teacup.

"Your
friend was
nervous because
she couldn't remember
what symptoms she should be looking
for," she said. "Now that I've lost my
pink stethoscope, this sort of thing will
be happening to vets all over the human
world."

"Is the pink stethoscope one of your
magical objects?" Rachel asked.

Heidi nodded.

"It helps vets to diagnose their patients' problems quickly," she said. "The green thermometer makes sure that all surgery equipment works well. The yellow blanket ensures that every poorly animal gets the care and comfort it needs to make it feel better. Without them, things are going to be very difficult for vets – and their patients."

"Do you have any idea where Jack Frost might have taken them?" asked Kirsty.

"They might be at his castle," said Heidi. "Erin the Firebird Fairy and I went there to search it, but it was too well guarded and we couldn't get in."

"Perhaps we should come with you to try again," said Rachel as she put the teacups on a tray. "We've been there quite a few times – we might be able to help you find a way in."

Kirsty added a plate of biscuits to the tray and picked it up.

"I'll take these through," she said. "When I come back, let's go to Fairyland straight away and search. After all, time will stand still here while we're away, so it won't cause trouble for Lisa."

Rachel and Heidi nodded, and Kirsty hurried to the waiting room with the tray. She handed the cups of tea around and offered everyone biscuits.

But when she reached the two short
journalists, they pushed her hand away.

"We don't like tea," said the first one in
a rude squawk.

"Yuck!" muttered the second, turning
away. "I want squashed-caterpillar
cordial."

Kirsty stared at them in astonishment.
They were keeping their heads down, but
she could see that both of them had long,
pointy noses.

"Oh no," she whispered to herself.
"They're goblins!"

She rushed back to the kitchen in a
flurry of excitement.

"There are goblins in the surgery!" she
exclaimed. "Those two short journalists
are goblins in disguise!"

"Oh my goodness!"
said Rachel. "I
suppose that
explains why
they were being
so rude."

Heidi's cheeks
had gone pink
with excitement.

"It explains
something else
as well," she said. "I

thought it was
strange that
the journalists
were able to
diagnose Maddie's
illness when the vet
couldn't. They must
have my magical
stethoscope!"

"Of course," said
Kirsty. "No goblin would ever know that
kind of information. The pink stethoscope
has made them able to tell what's wrong
with the patients. We have to get it back."

"But how?" asked Heidi.

"They must be carrying it in their
camera bag," Rachel guessed aloud. "It's
the only thing they have with them that
is big enough."

"The journalists still have their jackets
and bags in the waiting room," said
Kirsty. "Let's go and offer to take their
things to the cloakroom. Then we can
search the goblins' camera bag."

With Heidi safely hidden in Rachel's
tunic pocket, the girls hurried through to
the waiting room. Rachel

stepped forward
and faced the
journalists.

"Excuse me,
may we take
your bags or
coats?" she
asked the little
group. "I can
put them in the
cloakroom."

"Good idea," said the man who had taken their photo that morning. "You're both looking after us extremely well – thank you!"

One by one, the journalists handed them bags, jackets and briefcases. When the girls reached the goblins, they held their breath. Would their plan work?

Gifts for Goblins

To the girls' delight, the goblins seemed happy to hand over their camera bag. Rachel and Kirsty carried everything to the cloakroom. Heidi waved her wand and magically hung up all the coats, while the girls unzipped the camera bag.

"Is it there?" Heidi asked, hovering between them and clasping her hands together.

Rachel and Kirsty exchanged a disappointed look. Then Rachel turned the bag upside down and shook it.

"Nothing in there at all," she said. "They must have it with them – but where?"

"And how are we going to get it back?" asked Kirsty.

Rachel looked thoughtful.

"Goblins love new, sparkly things," she said. "Perhaps we could offer them something to replace the stethoscope.

It would have to be something that they would think was better."

"I've got just the thing," said Heidi with a wink.

She waved her wand and two stethoscopes were suddenly dangling from Kirsty's hand. They were bright green and glimmered like emeralds.

"Give them to the goblins," said Heidi. "Perhaps they will exchange them for my stethoscope."

Kirsty and Rachel went through to the waiting room. The goblin journalists were sitting in the far corner, next to a large plant pot.

"Excuse me, we've got a present for you," said Rachel. "It's a thank-you gift for being so clever about diagnosing Lisa's patient and helping her out."

Kirsty held out the stethoscopes.

"Green is the coolest colour for stethoscopes," she said. "All the other colours are very old-fashioned."

The goblins snatched them and put them in their ears without a word of thanks. Then they started listening to each other's heartbeat and giggling. As the girls watched, the tallest goblin reached up to his neck and tugged at something that was hidden under his shirt. Rachel squeezed Kirsty's hand as they watched him drop a pink stethoscope into the plant pot beside him.

"I don't want anyone saying I'm not fashionable," he muttered.

As soon as his back was turned, Kirsty pulled the pink stethoscope out of the plant pot. She tucked it under her tunic, but as she turned to leave the room, she stumbled. The pink stethoscope poked out from underneath her tunic – just as the goblins looked up at her.

Rachel and Kirsty froze. Everyone in the room thought that the goblins were journalists. If they accused the girls of stealing from them, they would probably be believed.

"Enjoy your trip?" asked the shorter goblin with a rude laugh.

"What a clumsy girl," said the taller goblin.

The girls breathed sighs of relief as Kirsty pushed the stethoscope out of sight. The goblins hadn't noticed it. They hurried back to the kitchen, where Heidi was waiting for them. When the little fairy saw her pink stethoscope, she did five cartwheels through the air.

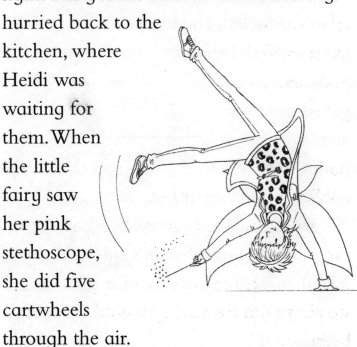

"You found it!" she exclaimed. "Oh, well done, Rachel and Kirsty. Thank you from the bottom of my heart!"

Kirsty handed it to her and it shrank to fairy size.

"Are you going to take it back to Fairyland?" asked Rachel.

Heidi nodded, and the girls were delighted to see her looking so happy.

"I'll be back very soon to help you keep an eye on the goblins," she promised. "After all, there are still two objects missing and I have to find them – with your help, of course!"

The Green Thermometer

Contents

Breakdown!

After Heidi left, Rachel and Kirsty were too busy to worry about what Jack Frost might be doing. Now they had found Heidi's pink stethoscope, Lisa was able to diagnose her patients properly. Animals were packed into the waiting room and Lisa was seeing them as quickly as she could. The journalists went back in to watch, and they were very impressed.

Rachel and Kirsty brought them trays of tea and biscuits, in between getting lunch ready. For now, everything was going well.

The only ones not smiling were the two goblins, who were still disguised as journalists.

"This is boring," the girls heard one of them squawk. "I wish that vet would make silly mistakes again – that was funny!"

As Rachel and Kirsty were putting plates of sandwiches on a table in the journalists' waiting room, they heard a loud crash.

"What was that?" Rachel exclaimed.

Someone cried out, and Kirsty's eyes grew wide.

"That was Lisa's voice," she said in alarm. "Oh Rachel, what do you think has happened?"

"I'll tell you what's happened," said Lisa, appearing in the doorway. "My most important piece of equipment has just broken, and I have no idea why."

Her chin wobbled as if she might be about to cry. The girls rushed over and put their arms around her.

67

"Everything seems to be going wrong this morning," she said, sniffing loudly. "It's a new machine – I can't understand why it would suddenly break. There's no way I'll be able to get an engineer out to fix it before this afternoon. How am I supposed to help my patients in the meantime?"

"We'll give the journalists their lunch while you ring the engineer," said Rachel. "Perhaps it won't be as bad as you think."

"Thanks, girls," she said. "I don't know what I would do without your help today."

Soon the journalists were back in the waiting room, munching on the sandwiches and drinking more tea. Rachel was collecting empty cups when she saw the goblins slipping outside. She hurried into the kitchen.

"Quick, Kirsty!" she whispered. "The goblins are up to something. Let's follow them!"

They found the goblins leaning against the railings and kicking the wall.

"I've had enough of hanging around here," the taller goblin was saying.

"Me too," agreed the second. "Shall we go back to Jack Frost's surgery?"

"I don't know," said the first goblin in a grumpy voice. "I bet he's still got those stupid other goblins in all the best jobs. I'd be a much better vet nurse than that short, spotty goblin."

"Anything's more fun than these boring humans," the other goblin replied.

"I hope Jack Frost's forgotten about us taking that stethoscope," said the first, sounding nervous.

"He'll be too busy thinking about where to steal his next patients from," said the other goblin. "All he cares about is making the fairies respect him. He won't even notice we're back. There aren't any interesting animals here. I bet Jack Frost has got loads of good ones from Heidi's surgery."

They scurried away down the street, and Rachel and Kirsty exchanged excited glances.

"So Jack Frost has kidnapped the patients to try to heal them," said Rachel. "He thinks that being a vet will make everyone respect him."

"But he doesn't know anything about being a vet!" said Kirsty. "We have to tell Heidi about this and save her patients. Come on – we're going to Fairyland!"

Travelling by Locket

The lockets that the girls wore were presents from the fairy queen, and there was just enough fairy dust inside for a journey to Fairyland. Rachel and Kirsty sprinkled the sparkling dust all over themselves.

"This is always so much fun!" said Kirsty, giggling as her body shrank to fairy size and gossamer wings grew from her back.

Rachel squeezed her hand.

"Please, fairy magic, take us to Heidi!" she said.

There was a whoosh of swirling fairy dust, and then they felt themselves being lifted into the air. When the sparkles cleared, they were standing outside a large white building, decorated with pictures of every animal imaginable. The sign above the door said:

Heidi was sitting on the front step beside Caitlin the Ice Bear Fairy, looking very gloomy indeed. When they saw Rachel and Kirsty, both fairies jumped to their feet in surprise and then rushed over to hug them.

"Hello!" Heidi exclaimed. "What are you both doing here?"

"We came to tell you that Jack Frost is trying to heal your patients in his surgery," said Kirsty. "We overheard the goblins talking about it."

"Oh my goodness, we have to find his surgery and rescue the animals," said Heidi. "While he has my magical objects, I can't help any new patients either. None of my equipment is working."

"One of Lisa's machines has broken, too," Rachel remembered.

"That's because the green thermometer is still missing," said Heidi. "Without it, all surgery equipment will stop working."

"May I come with you?" asked
Caitlin. "My pet bear Crystal is one of
the patients that Jack Frost stole. I'll do
everything I can to help find her!"

"Of course," said Kirsty. "Come
on, let's fly to the Ice Castle and start
searching for Jack Frost's surgery."

She knew how much Caitlin loved
Crystal. They had shared an adventure
together once before, when Jack Frost
had captured all the magical animals
and hidden them from their fairy friends.

It didn't take long to reach the icicle-
covered castle where Jack Frost lived.
Shivering, the four fairies fluttered above
the battlements and looked down.

"Look at all the goblin guards on
duty!" said Heidi. "However are we

going to get past them?"

"We know a few secret ways," Kirsty replied. "There's a trapdoor we could try …"

"Hold on!" said Rachel. "Look over there – beside the forest."

She pointed to the edge of the trees, where two goblins were just about to creep into the forest.

"Those goblins were at Lisa's surgery," said Kirsty. "They're still wearing their journalist disguises. They said they were going to find Jack Frost."

"Then we have to follow them!" cried
Caitlin.

The four friends zoomed after the
goblins and caught up with them a few
steps into the forest. The fairies fluttered
above the heads of the goblins as they
crashed and stumbled through the
bracken.

"Do you think they're lost?" asked Heidi eventually. "They've been walking for ages."

Just then, the goblins burst through a hedge into a clearing, where they headed towards a tall, round building made of stone. Outside it was a makeshift sign painted on a broken plank of wood:

Jack Frost
The Greatest Vet in the World!

"That's a folly," said Rachel, gazing at the building. "We've been reading about them at school. They're called 'follies' because foolish people build them to show off."

83

As soon as the goblin journalists had disappeared into the folly, the fairies swooped down and peered in through a window. Inside they could see a waiting room packed with poorly animals. The goblin receptionist was shuffling piles of paper, snapping at everyone and looking very muddled.

"I'll go and see what's through that window," said Kirsty.

She fluttered towards a window further along the round wall of the folly. When she peeped through, she gave a gasp of excitement and beckoned to the others.

"It's the examination room!" she whispered. "And Jack Frost is inside!"

An Exciting Discovery

There was a large portrait of Jack Frost hanging on the curved wall of the examination room. Jack Frost himself was examining a black cat, which was standing on a table holding one leg up in the air. A goblin in a white nurse's outfit was standing beside the table, clutching a green thermometer.

"That's my magical thermometer!" said Heidi, bobbing up and down in delight. "We've found it!"

"Aha, I see the problem," boomed Jack Frost at that moment. "I diagnose that this cat has ... a bad headache."

Heidi shook her head.

"Oh dear," she said in a worried voice. "That cat has a poorly knee, not a headache. It needs a bandage. This is terrible. The green thermometer will make sure that Jack Frost's equipment works, but without the pink stethoscope he won't be able to diagnose correctly."

"He might make the animals feel worse instead of better," said Caitlin. "We have to rescue them now!"

"*And* get the thermometer back," Rachel added.

Goblins were milling around the entrance to the folly, so they couldn't get in that way.

"Some follies have secret passages," Rachel said. "I wonder if Jack Frost has added any to this building."

"I hope so!" said Kirsty. "Where shall we look?"

"Let's fly in a wide circle around the folly," Caitlin suggested. "Look out for freshly dug earth — that would be a sign of a tunnel."

The fairies split up and flew high in the air so that the goblins below wouldn't spot them. They looked and looked, but they couldn't see anything to show recent digging.

Disappointed, Kirsty flew down and landed on a smooth rock. To her surprise, she saw that someone had set an iron ring into it.

"What a very strange rock," she said.

"It isn't a rock," Heidi exclaimed, landing beside her. "It's a slab – it's covering some sort of hole."

"A hole – or a tunnel," added Caitlin, as she and Rachel joined them on the slab. "Girls, we've found it!"

Together, the four fairies tugged hard at the iron ring. It was so heavy that they could hardly lift it, let alone use it to pull up the slab.

"We need some help," said Caitlin. "I know someone who lives nearby. Back in a minute!"

She zoomed off into the forest, and the others waited. For a few minutes, all they could hear were the squawks of squabbling goblins. There were no birds in this part of the forest — they were too scared of Jack Frost.

THUMP! THUMP! THUMP! Heavy footsteps were coming their way.

"What's that?" cried Rachel in alarm.

She and Kirsty grabbed each other's hands, but Heidi gave a little smile.

"I think I know," she said. "It's nothing to be scared of."

The bushes beside the stone slab rustled and trembled, and then a large brown snout poked through. It was followed by a big, shaggy bear, and Caitlin was riding on its back!

"Hi, everyone!" Caitlin smiled at the girls. "This is the slab I told you about," she said to the bear. "Do you think you could pull it open for us?"

"Of course," said the bear, smiling happily at them all. "Anything to help the fairies!"

The bear grasped the iron ring in her teeth and pulled. There was a scraping sound, and then the whole slab lifted up. Underneath was the entrance to a tunnel.

"Thank you," said the fairies together.

"My pleasure," said the bear.

She lumbered off into the forest again, and Rachel and Kirsty peered into the dark tunnel. It smelled of damp earth, and they felt very excited and a little bit anxious. What would they discover at the other end?

The Eyes of Jack Frost

The fairies fluttered along the passage in single file. Heidi was in the lead, and Caitlin was at the back. The tips of their wands glowed with golden light, so it was easy to see where they were going. But at the end of the passage, Heidi stopped so suddenly that Rachel almost flew into her.

"It's a dead end," said Heidi in a disappointed voice.

The others crowded forward to look. There was just a blank wall blocking the end of the passage.

"I wonder what those holes are for," said Kirsty.

She pointed to two holes high up on the wall. Rachel flew up and peeked through one of them.

"I can see the examination room!" she whispered. "Come and look!"

Kirsty joined her, and Heidi and Caitlin flew to the other hole. They could see that Jack Frost was now examining a monkey.

"I think this must be a secret door," said Heidi. "But I can't see how to open it."

"Even if we could open it, Jack Frost would be sure to notice," said Kirsty.

"I wonder why it has these holes in it," said Caitlin.

Kirsty let out a sudden gasp. "I think we're looking through that big portrait of Jack Frost that is hanging on the wall!" she said. "The holes must be his eyes. I bet he uses them for spying on the goblins when they think he's not around!"

"I've got an idea," said Rachel. "I think these holes are just big enough for us to squeeze through. They would notice if the whole door opened, but we might be able to get through the holes without being spotted and grab the thermometer."

Just then, the monkey scampered out of the room and a miniature pony trotted in.

"Hold it, stumpy legs," snapped Jack Frost. "I've still got to write up my important notes."

The fairies watched Jack Frost carefully. He had put down his stethoscope and thermometer so that the goblin nurse could wash them with all the other instruments. Everything was wheeled over to the sink on a small trolley.

"Let's slip out now while everything is being washed," Kirsty suggested, turning to the others. "Heidi, could you conjure up some more thermometers that look exactly the same as your magical one? Maybe we could swap them without being seen."

Heidi nodded, and the girls looked through the spy hole again. Jack Frost was hunched over his desk, scribbling his notes. He had his back to the portrait.

"Boring, boring, boring," they heard him grumbling to himself. "None of these animals has any sort of interesting illness."

"While Rachel and Kirsty try to get the thermometer, let's combine our magic to send all the animals back to your surgery," said Caitlin to Heidi.

"Good idea," Heidi whispered.

With a flick of her wand, she placed three green thermometers on the goblin nurse's trolley. Then the four fairies shared a hug.

"Good luck, everyone," said Heidi. "Let's go!"

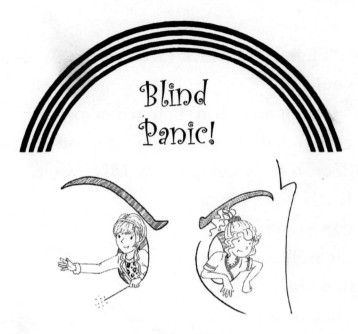

Blind Panic!

First Rachel, and then Kirsty, squeezed through one of the eyeholes, keeping their fingers crossed that Jack Frost wouldn't turn around. Heidi and Caitlin pushed their way through the other eyehole and winked at the surprised miniature pony. He let out a little whinny of joy and relief when he recognised Heidi.

"Quiet, you!" Jack Frost yelled. "Wait your turn!"

Caitlin and Heidi fluttered across the ceiling and slipped through the half-open door to the waiting room. Meanwhile, Rachel and Kirsty darted over to the trolley and hid underneath it. They kept their eyes on the goblin nurse, and watched him scratching his head.

"That's funny," he muttered. "I didn't think there were so many thermometers last time."

"Will you be quiet?" barked Jack Frost without turning around. "I'm a very busy, very important vet. I don't want to listen to you grumbling!"

The goblin stuck out his tongue behind Jack Frost's back and picked up one of the fake thermometers.

"This is our chance!" Rachel whispered as the goblin turned away to the sink.

The best friends zoomed upwards … just as Jack Frost finished writing his notes and turned around!

"Fairies!" he screeched. "Stop them!"

The goblin's mouth fell open. Kirsty managed to grab the green thermometer as Jack Frost hurled himself at the trolley. All his instruments crashed to the floor and Rachel and Kirsty darted back towards the portrait. Kirsty

squeezed through first, still clutching the thermometer. Rachel followed her, but halfway through she felt an icy hand grip her ankle.

"Jack Frost's got my foot!" she cried.

Kirsty tucked the thermometer into her pocket and held Rachel's hands, pulling as hard as she could.

"Let go!" shouted Jack Frost, sounding very cross indeed. "Give me back my thermometer!"

"It's not yours!" cried Rachel bravely.

"I can't hold on!" Kirsty exclaimed.

Rachel's hands started to slip away ...

and then the girls heard Heidi's voice.

"Oh no you don't!" exclaimed the little fairy.

Suddenly, Rachel felt Jack Frost let go of her ankle. She shot through the eyehole and whirled around to see what had happened. Jack Frost was staggering around the examination room, clawing at a blindfold that was covering  his eyes. Heidi and Caitlin zoomed back through the eyeholes, panting.

"Thank you!" Rachel exclaimed.

110

"We got back just in the nick of time!" said Caitlin. "Heidi used her magic to blindfold him."

"Thank goodness you did," said Kirsty, reaching into her pocket. "Here's your green thermometer, Heidi."

With a delighted sigh, Heidi took her precious thermometer.

"Now vets all over the human world will be able to use their equipment properly," she said. "And so will I!"

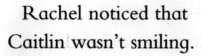

Rachel noticed that Caitlin wasn't smiling.

"Did you find Crystal?" she asked. "Is she all right?"

Caitlin shook her head sadly.

"She wasn't in the waiting room with the other animals," she said. "We've returned them all to Heidi's surgery, but poor Crystal is still missing."

"We'll find her, don't worry," said Kirsty with a kind smile. "But right now it's time to get out of here – before Jack Frost gets that blindfold off!"

The fairies flew back along the secret passage, away from the sound of Jack Frost stumbling around his examination room. Soon they were back in the forest.

Heidi hugged Rachel and Kirsty.

"You've been wonderful and brave," she said. "Thanks to you, my patients are back in my surgery and I can start to treat them."

"It's time for us to go back to Lisa's surgery," said Rachel. "But we haven't forgotten that your yellow blanket is still missing, Heidi. We'll do everything we can to help find it – and Crystal, of course."

"I'll see you both very soon," Heidi promised.

A tap of her wand filled the girls' lockets with fairy dust again, and then they were surrounded by a flurry of magical sparkles.

"Goodbye, Heidi!" they called.
"Goodbye, Caitlin! It's been a wonderful adventure!"

The Yellow
Blanket

Contents

Recovery
Room

The magical sparkles around Rachel and Kirsty faded, and they saw that they were standing outside Lisa's surgery. As usual, no time had passed in the human world since they had opened their lockets and travelled to Fairyland.

"Thank goodness we managed to find the green thermometer," said Kirsty.

"Now Lisa's equipment should start working again."

"Let's go and find out," said Rachel, heading back inside.

Lisa was just coming out of her examination room as the girls walked in. She greeted them with a big smile.

"Great news!" she said. "The machine has started working again, which means that I can work too. I still don't know what was wrong, but it looks as if I won't need the engineer after all."

Rachel and Kirsty exchanged happy smiles. They knew that the machine had started working again because Heidi had her green thermometer back.

"That's brilliant, Lisa," said Kirsty.

"I expect the journalists have nearly finished their lunch by now," Lisa added. "Would you like to join them while they look around the recovery room?"

"Yes, please!" said the girls together. They were really looking forward to meeting some new animals!

The girls cleared away the cups and plates from lunchtime, and then they led all the journalists to the door of the recovery room. Lisa was waiting for them there.

"This is the place where our animal patients stay while they get better after treatments and operations," said the young vet. "Let me tell you a little bit about what we have been doing to help them."

Lisa opened the door and led everyone inside as she started to describe the treatments that her patients had received.

"After a complicated operation, Isla is recovering well," she said, stroking the head of a tortoiseshell cat.

The girls were at the back of the group, and Kirsty was trying to listen, but

Rachel suddenly tugged on her arm.

"Listen to that dog," she said in a low voice.

Kirsty looked at a tubby little black-and-white dog who was curled up in a cat basket, next to a saucer of milk. A card placed next to her said 'Tess'. Kirsty bent down beside her.

"Hello, Tess," she said in a gentle voice.

To Kirsty's astonishment, the dog opened her mouth and let out a loud MIAOW! The dog next to her also started to miaow.

"Look over here," Rachel said, kneeling down beside the cats.

A beautiful cat called Smartie was wagging her tail and licking a bone!

"Something isn't right here," said Kirsty.

She stood up and glanced over at the journalists. They were still listening to Lisa and hadn't noticed the strange behaviour of the animals.

A few steps further along, Rachel noticed a budgie pecking at a carrot and a rabbit nibbling bird seed.

"Things are starting to go wrong again," said Rachel with a groan. "These animals all have the wrong food, and it's making them act strangely! The journalists are sure to notice something soon."

Lisa was still talking, but the journalists had also begun to take photographs.

"After the tour, I'll leave you to look around by yourselves," Lisa announced.

Rachel and Kirsty stayed beside the smaller animals as the tour moved on.

"This must be because the yellow blanket is still missing," Kirsty whispered. "Do you remember – Heidi said that it makes sure that poorly animals get the care they need?"

"That's right," said a tinkling voice beside them. "All poorly animals need special attention, but right now the animal food is getting all mixed up."

Inside a small cage labelled 'Chippie', Heidi the Vet Fairy was gently stroking the fur of a sleeping hamster.

Hide and Seek

The girls smiled at the caring fairy, and Heidi fluttered out through the bars of the cage.

"Good news – Chippie's doing really well," she said. "I just hope that there's some good news about my yellow blanket too."

"Do you have any idea where Jack Frost might have hidden it?" Rachel asked.

Heidi shook her head.

"It's still missing, and so is Crystal the ice bear," she said. "She must be Jack Frost's only patient, because we rescued all the others."

"Shall we go back to the folly surgery?" Kirsty suggested. "We could wait for a moment when Crystal is left alone."

But Heidi shook her head.

"I went back there, but it's empty," she said. "I couldn't find out where Jack Frost has taken Crystal. I've come to ask you to help me look for her."

"We want to help," said Rachel at once. "It's awful to think of little Crystal being all by herself. But we don't know where to look, and besides, I think Lisa might need us as well. The animals are in a terrible muddle. The cats are wagging their tails and the dogs are miaowing."

"Yes, I noticed that too," said Heidi. "I heard a gerbil quacking like a duck as well. It must be because of the missing blanket."

Just then, there was a loud thump above their heads. Rachel and Kirsty looked at each other in surprise.

"That's strange," said Kirsty, looking up at the ceiling. "There can't be anyone in the flat upstairs. Lisa told me that it isn't being used at the moment."

Kirsty saw a flash of excitement in Rachel's eyes. At exactly the same moment, she had an idea. Was it possible that Jack Frost was hiding right here in the surgery?

"Are you thinking what I'm thinking?" Rachel asked.

Kirsty nodded. The best friends understood each other so well that sometimes they didn't even need words! Rachel turned towards Heidi.

"We think that Jack Frost might be hiding upstairs," she said.

"Oh my goodness, that is *exactly* what he would do," said Heidi. "I expect he wants to steal Lisa's medicines."

"We need to go upstairs and check," said Kirsty. "We'll have to slip past the patients somehow."

"Heidi, could you turn us into fairies?" Rachel asked. "Then we could slip upstairs more easily."

Heidi nodded and the girls crouched down behind a large crate in the corner. The fairy swept her wand over their heads and they were dusted with magical sparkles. Instantly,

they shrank to fairy size and felt
gossamer wings unfurl
from their backs.
Then all three of
them fluttered
their wings
and rose
into the
air. The
journalists
were
listening to
Lisa talking
about the
more unusual
animals she had treated, and no one
spotted three little fairies swooping out of
the recovery room and back through the
surgery.

"The stairs are near the entrance," said Kirsty, "so we have to fly past the waiting room. Hopefully we won't be spotted!"

They hovered beside the entrance of the waiting room and peeped around the door. They could see four patients inside – a parrot, a kitten, a dog and a rabbit. Their owners were all chatting to each other.

"Come on," said Heidi. "No one's looking."

One by one they flew across the open doorway. Rachel and Heidi weren't spotted, but just as Kirsty crossed the doorway the dog looked up and let out a loud... MIAOW!

His owner looked embarrassed and Kirsty flitted out of sight, her heart pounding.

"That was close!" she said in a breathless voice. "Come on, the stairs are just over here."

The three friends zoomed up the narrow staircase to the first floor of the building. The painted white stairs were made of wood and did not have carpets.

"It's a good thing we're flying," said Rachel. "If Jack Frost is up there, he would hear us walking up these stairs."

As they reached the top of the stairs, they heard something and stopped in mid-air, hovering.

"That sounded like a voice," said Heidi.

"Not like that, you idiot!" they heard someone hiss.

"That's Jack Frost," said Kirsty. "We've found his hiding place!"

A Rescue Plan

The landing stretched out in front of the girls, and one of the doors along it was open. Rachel darted ahead and looked carefully around the doorway. Then she turned and beckoned to Kirsty and Heidi.

"Crystal's here," she whispered. "Come and see."

They hurried to join Rachel, and saw that the little ice bear was sitting on a yellow blanket in the centre of the room.

"That's my last magical object!" Heidi exclaimed, squeezing the girls' hands. "It's my yellow blanket."

Jack Frost was sitting on a chair gazing at Crystal. He was still wearing his white vet's coat, and he had a frown like thunder. He continued to snap out orders at lightning speed.

"Get some more cushions! Find my stethoscope! Give it some milk! Not *cold* milk, you nincompoop!"

Goblins were scurrying around him, trying to follow his orders and bumping into each other in a panic. As the fairies watched, one of the goblins offered Crystal some milk in a little bowl. The ice bear turned her head away, shivered and gave a little sneeze.

"Make her drink something!" Jack Frost barked. "She's obviously got sore toes and itchy fur. Drinking milk is the only cure." Heidi shook her head and frowned.

Kirsty and Rachel drew her away
from the door so that they could speak
without being heard.

"What do *you* think is wrong with
Crystal, Heidi?" asked Kirsty, feeling
anxious.

"It's just a mild cold," said Heidi. "I
have a tonic in my
surgery that
will cure her
straight away.
But Jack Frost
has no idea
what's wrong
with her, and
he can't do
anything to help."

"She must be feeling
poorly," said Rachel.

"Don't worry, she feels fine," said Heidi. "The yellow blanket will make sure that she gets the right care. It's lucky that Jack Frost has let her sit on it."

"But as long as the yellow blanket is in there, the animals downstairs will get the wrong food and act strangely," said Kirsty. "We have to get it back before the journalists notice that something's wrong."

"And we have to rescue Crystal so that Heidi can treat her," Rachel added. "But how on earth can we do either of those things? Jack Frost won't take his eyes off her, and there are goblins everywhere."

The fairies hovered close together, thinking hard.

"Perhaps we could trick them into leaving the surgery," Heidi suggested.

"But the only way out is down the stairs," said Kirsty. "The journalists and the patients would be sure to see them, and we can't let that happen."

"If we can't distract the goblins, perhaps we could distract Crystal," said Rachel. "She might be able to get away from

them – *if* we can make her understand
what we want her to do!"

Bear with a Blanket

Crystal knew Rachel and Kirsty from
their adventures with the Magical
Animal Fairies, and all the animals
in Fairyland knew and trusted Heidi
completely. They just had to make a plan
to reach the ice bear before they were
spotted by Jack Frost.

First, Heidi waved her wand at the window in the room where Jack Frost was sitting. It blew open and a warm breeze made the curtains flap.

"Shut that window!" Jack Frost shrieked at the goblins. "The ice bear must not be in any draughts!"

At that moment, everyone was staring at the window.

"Now, Rachel!" said Heidi in a whisper.

Rachel zipped across the room and tucked herself behind Crystal's fluffy ear. Kirsty and Heidi watched as she started to whisper to the ice bear.

"We just have to hope that Crystal will understand what to do," said Heidi.

"Yes, and that Jack Frost will let her do what she wants," Kirsty added. "Fingers crossed."

Hidden behind Crystal's ear, Rachel was having trouble making the sleepy ice bear pay attention to her.

"Dear Crystal, please try to remember me," she said. "My friend Kirsty and I met you last time Jack Frost hid you from Caitlin. We've come to help."

Crystal made a friendly snuffling noise.

"We need you to pick up the blanket and walk to the door," said Rachel. "Heidi is waiting for you, and she is going to take your cold away as soon as you get back to Fairyland. Will you help us and stand up?"

But Crystal shook her head. She was very cosy on the yellow blanket, and she didn't want to walk anywhere. Jack Frost was staring at her again, now that the goblins had closed the window.

"She needs sweets!" he declared suddenly. "Give her sweets NOW!"

The goblins rushed to some boxes

at the side of the room and pulled out
bags of sickly-looking green and yellow
candies. They tipped them into a
large bowl.

"Crystal, I know you feel a bit poorly,"
said Rachel. "But if you come with
me now, Heidi will make you better
again. And Caitlin is waiting for you in
Fairyland."

When Rachel mentioned Caitlin's
name, Crystal pricked up her ears. She
had been missing her special fairy friend
very much.

Slowly, Crystal got to her feet.

"Don't forget the blanket," Rachel reminded her.

Crystal picked up the yellow blanket in her teeth and took a couple of steps towards the door. The goblins all made an "oooh" sound.

"Shall we stop her?" one of them shouted.

"Leave her alone!" Jack Frost snapped.

"She's already feeling better, and that proves that I'm the greatest vet in the world. I cured her just by looking at her. *Praise me!*"

The goblins started to shout out wonderful things about Jack Frost, and all the time Crystal was ambling closer and closer to the door.

"You're the greatest!"

"Jack Frost forever!"

"Jack Frost is the king of vets!"

Suddenly Crystal stopped and sniffed the air. The goblin holding the sweets was nearby, and she could smell them.

"Come on, Crystal, we're nearly there," Rachel whispered in her ear. "You can do it!"

The goblins and Jack Frost watched as Crystal stepped onto the landing.

"Follow her," Jack Frost ordered.

But as soon as Crystal's back paws were on the landing, Heidi used her magic to shut the door with a loud SLAM!

Then she quickly spoke the words of a
locking spell.

"*Behind this door let Jack Frost stand
Until we're safe in Fairyland!*"

Adventure's End

"Get that door open!" Jack Frost yelled from inside the room.

The three fairies heard louds thumps and groans as the goblins threw themselves at the door. Heidi quickly turned Rachel and Kirsty back into humans. Then she picked up the yellow blanket and stroked Crystal's soft head.

The blanket and the ice bear shrank back to fairy size.

"I must return to Fairyland now," Heidi said as Crystal nuzzled her arm. "How can I ever thank you for all your help? It's been an amazing day, and I have my magical objects back again. You've saved animals and vets all over the human world and Fairyland!"

"We're just glad we could help," said Kirsty.

"Now I'll take Crystal to my surgery and give her the tonic," Heidi went on. "She'll soon be completely well again."

Heidi swept her wand through the air, and then she and Crystal disappeared in a flurry of gold and silver fairy dust. At that moment, the girls heard Jack Frost yelling again.

"Stand aside!" he bellowed. "I'll blast that door open with a thunderbolt!"

Amid the squawks of terrified goblins, there was a loud bang and a bright-blue flash. Then the door burst open and Jack Frost marched out, looking very cross indeed.

"Where's the bear?" he demanded, spotting the girls. "Where's the blanket?"

Rachel reached for Kirsty's hand.

"Crystal and the blanket are back where they belong," she said bravely. "Heidi has taken them to Fairyland. Your naughty tricks are over."

"No! No! NO!" Jack Frost shouted, clutching his spiky hair and jumping up and down on the spot. "You wretched interfering humans!"

"If you keep taking things that don't belong to you, we will keep stopping you," said Kirsty. "You should leave the poorly animals alone."

"I don't want anything more to do with any poorly animals!" said Jack Frost in a temper. "I'm going to knock that stupid folly down and I never want to hear the word 'vet' again!"

He stamped his foot, and there was a dazzling flash of blue light. Then Jack Frost and all the goblins had gone. The girls heard footsteps clattering up the wooden stairs, and then Lisa came hurrying towards them.

"Girls, what was that loud bang?" she asked. "Are you OK?"

"We're fine," said Rachel. "Don't worry."

"Well, you shouldn't really be up here," said Lisa. "Come back downstairs – the journalists are looking around the surgery and they all seem really impressed. It's going well!"

"How are all the animals in the recovery room?" asked Kirsty as they followed Lisa back down the stairs.

"They're doing really well," said Lisa. "Recovering just as they should."

Back down in the surgery, the journalists were walking around, taking pictures and smiling.

"This is a wonderful surgery," said one woman to Lisa. "I'll be writing that your ideas are the future for vets."

Rachel and Kirsty hugged each other as Lisa looked at her watch.

"It's almost the end of the day," she said. "Time to start tidying up, girls. Would you go and bring the balloons in, please?"

Outside by the railings, Kirsty smiled at her best friend.

"This is where our whole adventure started," she said. "I'm so happy that we were able to find Heidi's magical objects. I hope Crystal will be all right now."

"Of course she will," said Rachel as she started to untie the balloons. "Heidi knows exactly how to look after her. And

do you want to know something else, Kirsty? I have a feeling that Lisa's surgery is going to be a huge success!"

Now it's time for Kirsty and Rachel to help...

Julia

the Sleeping Beauty Fairy

Read on for a sneak peek...

Rachel Walker rested her hand on the drawbridge chain of Tiptop Castle and looked down at the moat below. Her best friend, Kirsty Tate, was standing beside her, gazing at the elegant lawns and flower gardens that surrounded the castle. They had paused halfway across the drawbridge to admire the view.

"I feel like a princess standing here," said Kirsty in a dreamy voice. "It's just like something out of a fairy tale!"

"We're so lucky to be able to stay here

for the Fairytale Festival," said Rachel, as the spring breeze ruffled her blonde hair.

It was half term, and Kirsty was staying with Rachel to share a very special treat. Tiptop Castle was a beautiful old castle on the edge of Tippington, and this year it was hosting the famous Fairytale Festival.

"I can't wait to see all the people dressed up as fairies and fairytale characters," said Kirsty.

"I wonder if we'll meet any real fairies," said Rachel.

The girls shared a happy smile. They had been friends of the fairies ever since they met on Rainspell Island, and had shared many amazing adventures.

"Come on," said Kirsty. "Let's go inside."

The castle gatehouse was decorated

with glimmering fairy lights. Inside was a festival organiser dressed as Puss-in-Boots. He waved his paw at Kirsty and Rachel, and then stroked his whiskers.

"Welcome to Tiptop Castle!" he said in a deep voice. "What are your names?"

The girls told him, and he ticked them off on his list. Then he gave them a big smile.

"Please enter the castle and explore with the other children until lunchtime," he said. "You can go anywhere you like and look at everything. Have fun!"

"This is going to be amazing!" said Rachel, hurrying inside and gazing around the grand entrance hall.

A chandelier hung from the ceiling, thickly crusted with glittering diamonds. Twinkling fairy lights were twined around the banisters of a gigantic staircase, and suits of armour lined the walls.

"Where shall we look first?" asked Kirsty.

"Let's go upstairs," said Rachel, seizing her best friend's hand. "I want to see what a princess's bedroom looks like!"

Giggling, the girls ran up the staircase and discovered a long, wide corridor. All the doors were open, and they peeped inside all of them, gasping at what they saw. Each room was decorated in a different way. Rachel's favourite had golden furniture and red velvet curtains, while the one Kirsty liked best had a silver four-poster bed in the centre. It was surrounded by gauzy drapes and topped with a thick canopy of ivory satin. The curtains at the tall windows were azure blue.

"It looks like a mermaid's bedroom," she said with a happy sigh. "Look — the mirror is encrusted with tiny silver seashells!"

Read **Julia the Sleeping Beauty Fairy** to find out what adventures are in store for Kirsty and Rachel!

Join in the magic online by signing up
to the Rainbow Magic fan club!

Meet the fairies, play games and
get sneak peeks at the latest books!

There's fairy fun for everyone at

www.rainbowmagicbooks.co.uk

You'll find great activities, competitions, stories and
fairy profiles, and also a special newsletter.

Find a fairy with
your name!